Introducing Pop Monsters...

Deep in the heart of the Pacific Northwest there lives a furry band of critters that come in all shapes and sizes. In that wooded glen, among the misty meadows and mossy-bearded trees, they share fun and adventure in a magical place called Wetmore Forest.

STERLING CHILDREN'S BOOKS
New York

An Imprint of Sterling Publishing Co., Inc.
1166 Avenue of the Americas
New York, NY 10036

ISBN 978-1-4549-3486-8

Distributed in Canada by Sterling Publishing Co., Inc.
c/o Canadian Manda Group, 664 Annette Street
Toronto, Ontario M6S 2C8, Canada
Distributed in the United Kingdom by GMC Distribution Services
Castle Place, 166 High Street, Lewes, East Sussex BN7 1XU, England
Distributed in Australia by NewSouth Books, University of New South Wales
Sydney, NSW 2052, Australia

For information about custom editions, special sales, and premium and corporate purchases, please contact Sterling Special Sales at 800-805-5489 or specialsales@sterlingpublishing.com.

Manufactured in China
Lot #:
2 4 6 8 10 9 7 5 3 1
06/19

BUGSY SAVES THE DAY

A ·WETMORE FOREST· STORY

By Randy Harvey and Sean Wilkinson

Illustrated by John Skewes

STERLING CHILDREN'S BOOKS

New York

One day in Wetmore Forest, Bugsy found Tumblebee sitting at the base of a mushberry bush with a terrible tummy ache. When it came to snacking on mushberries, Tumblebee often didn't know when to stop. Bugsy decided he'd better get help.

"Tumblebee, you stay put!" said Bugsy. "I'll go get
Sapwood Mossbottom. He'll fix you right up."

Sapwood Mossbottom was the wise elder and
healer of Wetmore Forest, and Bugsy knew that
he would have a remedy to make Tumblebee's
belly better.

Bugsy told Mossbottom about
Tumblebee's tummy troubles.

"Oh, he does love his mushberries, doesn't he?" said Mossbottom as he stirred a pot on the stove. "I shall prepare a special mix of roots and herbs to ease his tummy."

"Hmmm, seems I'm out of Pitter-pat root!" said Mossbottom. "This just won't do. Bugsy, you must fly to Bogwoller Swamp, the only place where Pitter-pat roots grow, and bring me one for the mix."

"But Bogwoller Swamp is so far away! And I'm not sure my wings are big and strong enough to fly such a long way . . . I'm more of a glider than a flyer."

"You can do it, Bugsy," said Mossbottom. "I believe in you, and Tumblebee is counting on you. Look for the blue flower with three petals and pull it up by the root. Then bring it here as fast as your wings can carry you."

Bugsy flew on, thinking to himself, *I wish I was more like my dad. He had great big wings, and they say he could fly all the way to Mount Shuksan and back without any trouble at all.*

Just then, Bugsy noticed dark storm clouds gathering in the sky overhead.

He gulped. Bugsy didn't like thunder. When he
was small, he used to hide under his mom's wing
whenever thunderstorms came. He wanted to hide
now, too.

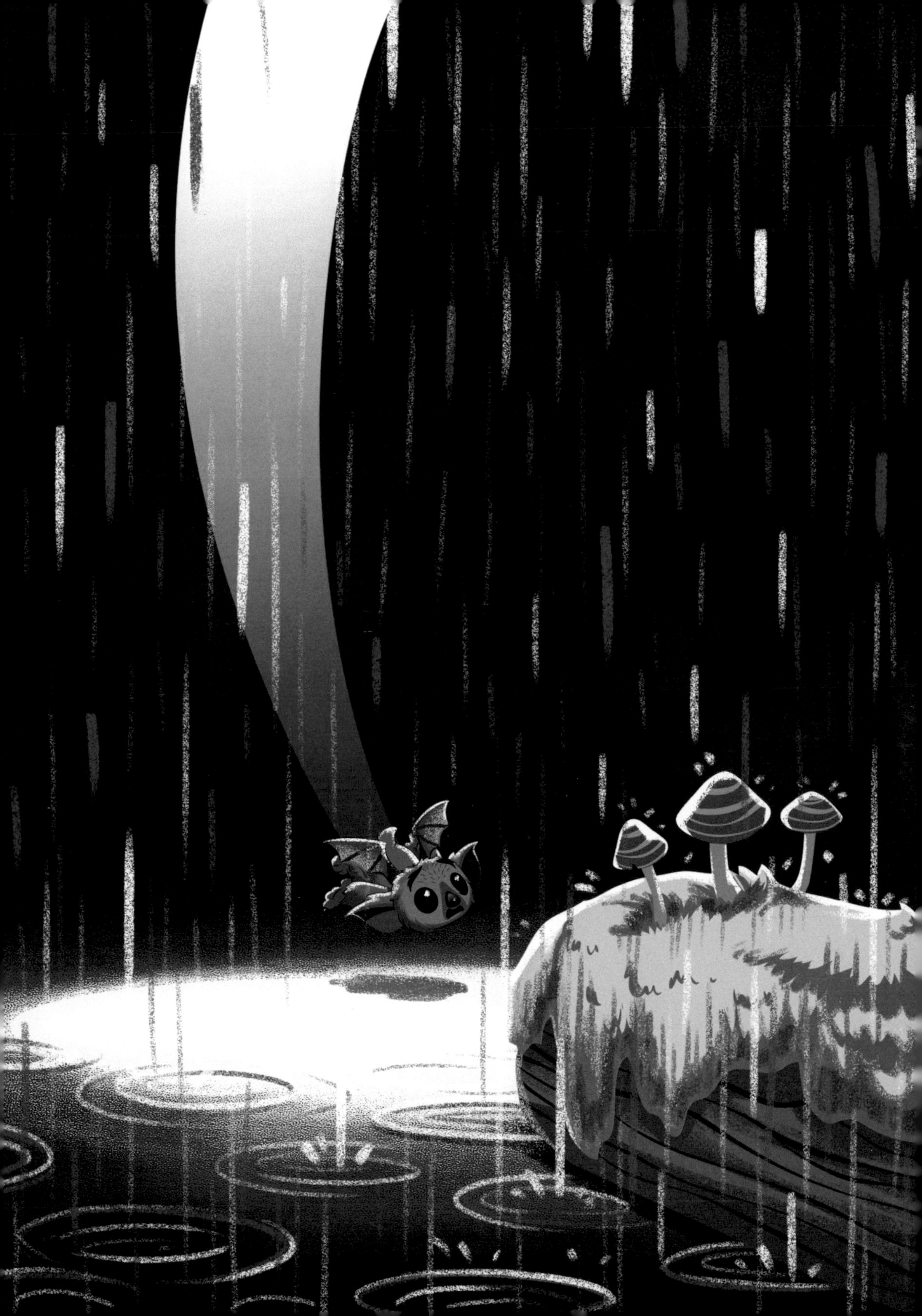

Bugsy always felt safest in the hollow of a log or a cozy cave, away from the rain and wind and lightning. He was the littlest of all his monster friends. They always looked out for him and kept him safe.

But he knew he couldn't hide from the thunder
this time. "I've got to get that Pitter-pat root!
I've got to get it for Tumblebee!"

"I made it!"
Bugsy said proudly.

"Now, to find the Pitter-pat root and fly it back to Mossbottom. . . ."

"You did it Bugsy! I knew you could," said Mossbottom as he added the root to his boiling pot. "I'll add a drop of bimble-bee honey to make it taste better. Now the mixture is ready. Soon Tumblebee will be feeling fit as a fiddle-fern shoot."

In no time at all, Tumblebee was
back to his old self again.

"Good job, Bugsy!" his friends cheered.

"Yes, your little wings saved the day!"

Mossbottom said to Bugsy.

"Your dad would be very proud."